Farm Animals

Working Dogs

Sharon Dalgleish

CHELSEA CLUBHOUSE
An Imprint of Chelsea House Publishers
A Haights Cross Communications Company
Philadelphia

This edition first published in 2005 in the United States of America by Chelsea Clubhouse, a division of Chelsea House Publishers and a subsidiary of Haights Cross Communications.

Chelsea House Publishers
2080 Cabot Boulevard West, Suite 201
Langhorne, PA 19047-1813

The Chelsea House world wide web address is www.chelseahouse.com

First published in 2005 by
MACMILLAN EDUCATION AUSTRALIA PTY LTD
627 Chapel Street, South Yarra, Australia, 3141

Associated companies and representatives throughout the world.

Visit our website at www.macmillan.com.au

Library of Congress Cataloging-in-Publication Data

Dalgleish, Sharon.
Working dogs / Sharon Dalgleish.
p. cm. -- (Farm animals)
Includes index.
ISBN 0-7910-8275-X
1. Working dogs--Juvenile literature. I. Title.
SF428.2.D35 2005
636.73--dc22

2004016193

Edited by Ruth Jelley
Text and cover design by Christine Deering
Page layout by Domenic Lauricella
Photo research by Legend Images
Illustration by Luke Jurevicius

Printed in China

Acknowledgments
Special thanks to Andy Carpenter and the hard-working Betsy.
The author and the publisher are grateful to the following for permission to reproduce copyright material:

Cover photograph: New Zealand Hunter at work, courtesy of © Peter E. Smith, Natural Sciences Image Library.

Australian Picture Library/Corbis, pp. 25 (top), 28; Corbis Digital Stock, p. 30; The DW Stock Picture Library, pp. 6, 8 (bottom), 10 (top), 11 (center), 16, 17, 24 (top); Getty Images, pp. 9, 12; © Peter E. Smith, Natural Sciences Image Library, pp. 1, 24 (bottom), 25 (bottom); Pelusey Photography, pp. 4, 13, 15, 20, 23; Photodisc, pp. 3, 7, 8 (top), 18; Photolibrary.com, pp. 5, 8 (center); Photolibrary.com/Animals Animals, pp. 10 (bottom), 11 (top and bottom); Photolibrary.com/SPL, p. 14; David Hancock/Skyscans, pp. 19, 26, 27.

Contents

What Is a Working Dog?

A working dog is like any other dog. But a working dog is not a pet. Working dogs are kept by farmers to do farmwork.

A working dog waits for the farmer's command.

The adult female dog is called a bitch. The adult male is called a dog. The young are called pups. A group of dogs is called a pack.

A farmer usually has more than one working dog.

Built for Work

Working dogs are built to run fast. They can run for a long time and over a long distance.

Like other dogs, working dogs have a good sense of smell.

Working dogs are bred to be clever and to love work. They use their **instincts** to round up **livestock** such as sheep.

The farmer and the dog work together to round up livestock.

Life Cycle

Pups grow up to have pups of their own, and the life cycle continues.

Pups are born with their eyes and ears closed. They open their eyes when they are 10 to 14 days old.

Pups leave their mother when they are about eight weeks old.

Adult dogs and bitches **mate** to produce pups. Most farmers wait until a bitch is two years old before letting her have pups.

Pups

Pups cannot see or hear when they are very young, but they can smell. They smell their mother and crawl around to drink milk from her.

Looking after the pups is hard work for the mother.

Growing Up

When pups are three months old, they will start training to work on the farm.

Day 1

The pups are born with their eyes and ears closed.

At about 2 weeks

The pups begin to see and hear.

At about 3 weeks

The pups can walk and explore on their own.

At about 6 weeks

The pups are ready to stop drinking their mother's milk.

At about 12 weeks

The pups are ready to learn about farm work.

Farm Life

Working dogs wake up early in the morning before the farmer starts work. They often follow the farmer around all day, keeping him or her company as the chores are done.

A working dog goes with the farmer to do the daily chores.

The dogs also have work to do on the farm. They work hard. They might spend the day **mustering** horses, or rounding up sheep or cattle with the farmer.

Working dogs help the farmer to round up the sheep.

Eating

Like all dogs, working dogs eat their food quickly. Dogs don't have as many **taste buds** as people. They are attracted to the smell of the food, not the flavor.

Like other dogs, working dogs chew bones.

When people eat, **digestion** starts in the mouth as the food is chewed and mixed with saliva. Dogs use saliva to help them swallow their food whole. Digestion begins in their stomach.

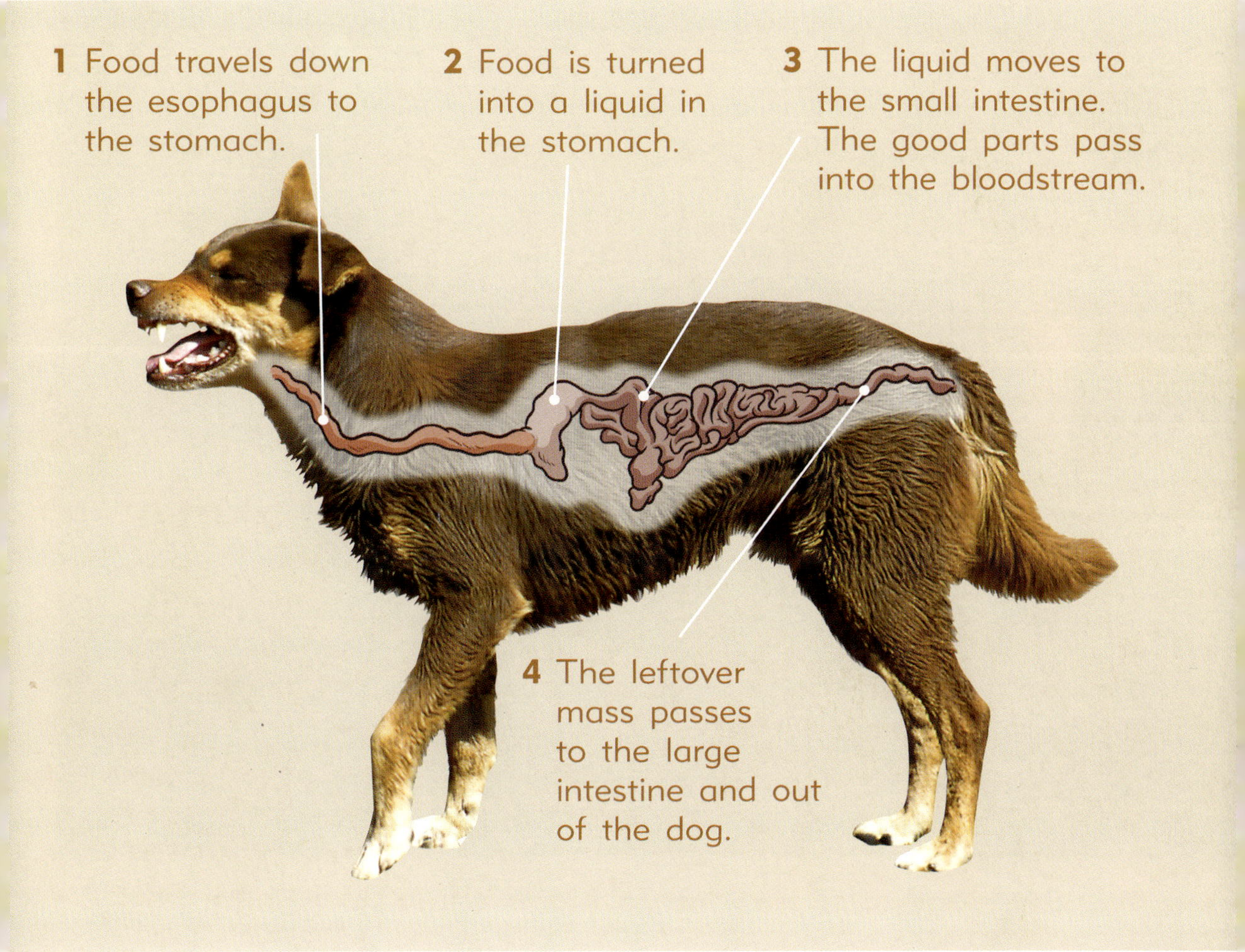

Playing

Working dogs don't have time to play. They are too busy working with the farmer. But when they have done their work, they may cool off with a swim.

Working dogs often cool off in a water hole or trough.

Sleeping

Working dogs do not sleep inside the farm house. At the end of the day they find a sheltered spot outside to sleep. They are still on duty, keeping watch.

Working dogs sometimes sleep in a kennel outside.

Dogs at Work

Most sheep farms have working dogs. The farmer signals to the dog by whistling or calling. The dog can recognize the farmer's signals and knows what the farmer wants it to do.

Working dogs walk around the livestock.

Cattle and dairy farms usually have dogs, too. The dogs help round up and move the cattle from field to field. They also help control the cattle in the yards.

Working dogs nip at the cattle's heels to make them move.

Training

It's a lot of hard work to train a farm dog. The farmer often starts by letting the pup follow on walks. Then the pup practices with just a few sheep in a yard.

Young dogs are trained on a short rope, then a long rope, and finally no rope.

When the dog is about six months old, the farmer can teach it basic commands. The first commands taught are "come" and "sit." The older dogs help teach the young dogs.

Command	What It Means
come	come to me
get over, or come by	move clockwise around the livestock
good dog	that is correct
sit	sit down or stop right there
steady	slow down
uh, uh	that is wrong
walk in	approach the livestock steadily
way to me	move counterclockwise around the livestock

Hand Signals

Working dogs can also learn hand signals from the farmer. The command "get over" can be used with a right-hand signal. This tells the dog to move clockwise around the livestock.

The farmer tells the dog to move clockwise around the sheep.

Dog Trials

Some farmers enter their dogs in competitions, called trials. The trials test a working dog's training and instincts. Dogs are judged on how well they complete an everyday farm task.

At trials, dogs complete tasks such as rounding up sheep.

Working Dog Breeds

Different working dog **breeds** have different skills.

The Australian Kelpie is a smart dog that is popular on sheep farms.

The Border Collie is a popular sheep dog in Australia and North America.

Some working dogs gather sheep in rolling fields. Some work cattle over huge areas. Some even herd reindeer!

The Rough Collie is popular in North America.

The New Zealand Huntaway is different from most other herding dogs. It barks while it works.

Looking After Working Dogs

Farmers look after working dogs by keeping them fit and healthy. They make sure there is enough water for the dogs to drink throughout the day.

Working dogs drink water from troughs or wherever they can.

Sometimes farmers might need to call a **vet** if a dog is sick or needs **vaccinations**. Farmers may also need to **groom** their dogs, to keep their fur and skin healthy.

Farmers groom their dogs with a brush.

Farm Safety

Farmers need to keep their working dogs safe around tractors, motorbikes, and other farm machinery. Working dogs must obey the farmer's whistles to stay out of danger.

Farmers check where a dog is before moving a tractor or motorbike.

How to Whistle a Working Dog

Try making these whistles that a working dog is trained to obey.

1 Change the notes as you whistle by making your lips tighter or looser, or by curling your tongue.

2 The whistle must be loud so that the dog can hear it.

Whistle Sound	What It Means
Loud PHEEWIT	come here
PHEW, long whistle that goes down at the end	sit or stop
PHERR, in a long steady note	steady, slow down
SWIT SWIT, two short whistles	walk in to livestock
WHEET-WHEEEO, going up at the end	get over, or move clockwise
WHEE-WHOO, going down at the end	way to me, move counterclockwise

Farm Facts

- Dogs can hear sounds ten times farther away than people can. They can move their ears around to pick up sounds from many directions.

- Many dogs move their lips, lick, and chew while they sleep. Some move their feet like they are running or swimming. Some even growl, whine, or wag their tails. They are probably dreaming.

- The common belief that dogs are color blind is not true. Dogs can tell the difference between blue, yellow, and gray. They probably do not see red or green. This is much like a person's vision is at twilight.

Glossary

breed a group of animals that have the same set of features

digestion the process that breaks down food

groom to clean an animal's fur

instinct natural tendency or behavior

livestock animals farmed for food, such as cattle and sheep

mate when a male and female join to create their young

mustering gathering animals together

taste bud part of the tongue used for taste

vaccination medicine injected into animals to protect them from disease

vet a doctor who treats animals

Index